Welcome to ALADDIN QUIX!

If you are looking for fast, fun-to-read stories with colorful characters, lots of kid-friendly humor, easy-to-follow action, entertaining story lines, and lively illustrations, then **ALADDIN QUIX** is for you!

But wait, there's more!

If you're also looking for stories with tables of contents; word lists; about-the-book questions; 64, 80, or 96 pages; short chapters; short paragraphs; and large fonts, then **ALADDIN QUIX** is *definitely* for you!

ALADDIN QUIX: The next step between ready to reads and longer, more challenging chapter books, for readers five to eight years old.

TO THE RESCUE

Read more ALADDIN QUIX books!

By Stephanie Calmenson

Our Principal Is a Frog!
Our Principal Is a Wolf!
Our Principal's in His Underwear!
Our Principal Breaks a Spell!
Our Principal's Wacky Wishes!
Our Principal Is a Spider!

Little Goddess Girls
By Joan Holub and Suzanne Williams

Book 1: *Athena & the Magic Land*
Book 2: *Persephone & the Giant Flowers*
Book 3: *Aphrodite & the Gold Apple*
Book 4: *Artemis & the Awesome Animals*

Mack Rhino, Private Eye
By Jennifer Swender and Paul DuBois Jacobs

Book 1: *The Big Race Lace Case*
Book 2: *The Candy Caper Case*

Geeger the Robot
By Jarrett Lerner

Book 1: *Geeger the Robot Goes to School*
Book 2: *Geeger the Robot Lost and Found*

GEEGER THE ROBOT

TO THE RESCUE

CHEER UP!

ILLUSTRATED
BY
Serge
Seidlitz

ALADDIN QUIX

New York   London   Toronto   Sydney   New Delhi

ALADDIN QUIX
Simon & Schuster Children's Publishing Division
1230 Avenue of the Americas, New York, New York 10020
First Aladdin QUIX paperback edition September 2021
Text copyright © 2021 by Jarrett Lerner
Illustrations copyright © 2021 by Serge Seidlitz
Also available in an Aladdin QUIX hardcover edition.
All rights reserved, including the right of reproduction in whole or in part in any form.
ALADDIN and the related marks and colophon are registered
trademarks of Simon & Schuster, Inc.
For information about special discounts for bulk purchases, please contact
Simon & Schuster Special Sales at 1-866-506-1949 or business@simonandschuster.com.
The Simon & Schuster Speakers Bureau can bring authors to your live event. For
more information or to book an event contact the Simon & Schuster Speakers Bureau
at 1-866-248-3049 or visit our website at www.simonspeakers.com.
Book designed by Karin Paprocki
The illustrations for this book were rendered digitally.
The text of this book was set in Archer Medium.
Manufactured in the United States of America 0821 OFF
2 4 6 8 10 9 7 5 3 1
Library of Congress Control Number 2021939431
ISBN 978-1-5344-8023-0 (hc)
ISBN 978-1-5344-8022-3 (pbk)
ISBN 978-1-5344-8024-7 (ebook)

For Blair and Justin,

my very first friends

Cast of Characters

Geeger: a very hungry robot

DIGEST-O-TRON 5000: a machine that turns the food Geeger eats into electricity

Ms. Bork: Geeger's teacher

Fudge: the class hamster

Sidney, Arjun, Olivia, Mac, Suzie, Raul, Gabe, Roxy: kids in Geeger's class

Tillie: a student at Geeger's school, and Geeger's best friend

Contents

1

Zip! Zip! Zip!

Geeger is a robot. A very, very hungry robot.

Geeger was **constructed** in a laboratory by a team of scientists. Then he was sent to the town of Amblerville, where he eats all the food that the rest of the towns-people don't want.

Rotten eggs, moldy bread, mushy fruit—all that and then some!

Geeger has a brain, just like you. There's one BIG difference, though. Geeger's brain is made up of wires, while your brain is made up of . . . well, gooey brain stuff.

Most of the time, Geeger's brain tells him to do just one thing:

EAT! EAT! EAT! EAT! EAT!

At the end of every day, Geeger plugs himself into his **DIGEST-O-TRON 5000.** The machine sucks up all the food that Geeger has eaten—*SLUUUURP!*—and turns it into electricity. The electricity then helps power Amblerville!

Now and again, Geeger gets confused and eats things he's not supposed to . . .

Like forks, batteries, and toaster ovens.

When Geeger does that, the

DIGEST-O-TRON lets him know. The machine's lights flash. Its sirens scream. **WEE-oOoOo! WEE-oOoOo! WEE-oOoOo!**

But it's been several weeks since Geeger has made the DIGEST-O-TRON flash and scream. The robot has been getting very good at only eating things he's supposed to eat.

Speaking of weeks—it wasn't too many weeks ago that Geeger made a **BIG** decision. . . .

He decided to start going to school!

Geeger *loves* going to Amblerville Elementary School. Every single day, he learns something new. Some days, Geeger learns *a whole bunch* of new things! On those days, he can just about feel the wires in his brain **pulsing** with electricity.

Zip!

Zip!

ZiiiIiIiIiIIIP!

Geeger's teacher is named **Ms. Bork**. Geeger loves spending time in Ms. Bork's classroom. There's the class pet, **Fudge**—the fuzziest, cuddliest hamster in the history of hamsters.

Plus, the room is full of books—Geeger LOVES books—and the walls are covered in student artwork. Even Geeger has a work of art hanging up!

But as much as Geeger likes it in Ms. Bork's classroom, there's one place in Amblerville Elementary

School that Geeger might like to be even more.

The cafeteria.

What a place!

It's big and noisy. It's **brimming** with mouthwatering, circuit-sizzling scents. It's full of **FOOD**!

But Geeger's favorite thing about the cafeteria is that there's only one thing kids (and robots!) are supposed to do there:

EAT! EAT! EAT! EAT! EAT!

And so Geeger steps through the doors of the cafeteria, finds a seat at his usual table, and prepares to do exactly that.

2

Lunchtime

The first thing Geeger and his friends always do at lunch is share what they brought with them to eat.

Today, **Sidney** arrives and sits down first.

She holds up something square-shaped and wrapped in shiny silver foil, plus a little bag of something green and flaky.

"Pickle and mayonnaise sand- 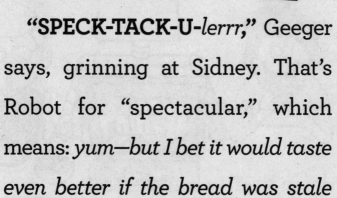 wich with a side of seaweed," she says.

"SPECK-TACK-U-*lerrr*," Geeger says, grinning at Sidney. That's Robot for "spectacular," which means: *yum—but I bet it would taste even better if the bread was stale* *and the mayonnaise was expired!*

Arjun shows up next.

He holds up a clear plastic container filled with something stringy and red, plus a bag of sticky-looking pellets.

"Leftover spaghetti and meat-balls and a side of dates," he says.

"SPIFF-eee," Geeger says, giving Arjun a thumbs-up. That's Robot for "spiffy," which means: *super yummy—but I bet it would taste even better if the spaghetti was moldy!*

One by one the rest of Geeger's

friends show up and sit down. **Olivia** has a stack of crackers, a hunk of cheddar cheese, and a few squares of chocolate.

Mac has hard-boiled eggs, a jar of pickled vegetables, and a bunch of pretzels.

Suzie and **Raul** both brought pizza—Suzie's has mushroom and onion on it, and Raul's has pineapple and pepper.

Gabe has a bologna sandwich on rye bread, and **Roxy** has a grilled cheese loaded up with *four* different kinds of mustard.

"SPLEN-*diiid*,**"** Geeger says, winking at all his friends. That's Robot for "splendid," which means: *holy cow does that look yummy—but I bet it would all taste even better if you left it in a dumpster for a couple weeks!*

As soon as Roxy is done sharing, she and all the rest of the kids from Ms. Bork's class turn their attention to Geeger. They are eager to see what *he* brought for lunch.

Geeger reaches for his lunch box, but stops when he **realizes** something.

Tillie.

His best friend.

She hasn't shared what *she* brought for lunch yet.

Geeger looks to his left, since Tillie always sits right beside him at lunch.

But she's not there.

"TILL-*eee*?" says Geeger.

"Hmmf."

The sound comes from the far end of the table. Geeger has to lean forward to get a look. And there he sees Tillie, slumped over her lunch, her lips sagging down in a frown.

"Bagel...," she mutters. "Cream cheese..."

Geeger can see that Tillie is unhappy. Even if he *wasn't* her best friend, he would be able to tell just by looking at her. Did she not want a bagel with cream cheese for lunch?

Before he can ask her, Gabe says, **"Come on, Geeger!** Hurry up and show us what you've got!"

Geeger keeps his eyes on Tillie. He watches her pick up her

bagel, tear off a tiny bite, then drop the rest of the thing atop the baggie that it came in.

"Geeger!" cries Gabe. "Come on already!"

"OH-*kaaay***, OH-***kaaay***,"** Geeger says, grabbing his lunch box. He prepares to show his friends what *he* brought for lunch.

3

Brrriingggg!

"LET US *seeee,"* Geeger says. He pops open the lid of his lunch box and wiggles his fingers over the assortment of spoiled and rotten and stale and expired food inside.

He removes the items, one by
one, and sets them on the table
before him.

He has:

- six slices of bread (moldy)
- nine clementines (even moldier)

- 27 crackers (stale)
- 22 carrots (slimy and expired)
- three zucchinis (rotten)
- 11 slices of Gruyère cheese (stinky)
- 19 cubes of Gouda cheese (*beyond* stinky)
- three blocks of Gorgonzola cheese (so stinky it was deemed hazardous by the Amblerville Department of Public Health)
- one package of chocolate pudding (expired)

"AND . . . ," Geeger adds, plucking one last item out of his lunch box. "ONE af-TER *lunch* MINT, *sooo* **OLD it is PRAC-tic-ULL-***eee* **AYN-chint.**"

"Oooh," says Gabe. "An **ancient** mint." Then he takes a giant bite of bologna and rye bread.

Geeger sees his friend eating the sandwich, and his brain goes bananas.

EAT! EAT! EAT! EAT! EAT! it tells him.

Geeger doesn't hesitate.

He scoops up a pair of moldy clementines. The first he tosses into his mouth. The second he shoves directly through the door in his stomach.

Next Geeger reaches for some cheese.

And the rest of the period zips by in a delicious blur.

Before Geeger knows it, he hears a *brrrRRRIIINNNNG!*

It's the bell, **signaling** the end of lunch.

Half a second after it rings, all the kids in the cafeteria are on their feet. They clean off their tables, throw away their trash, recycle their **recyclables**, and head for the exit.

Geeger is right there with them, **striding** along between Olivia and Gabe. He's just about through

the door when he realizes something that stops him short.

Tillie.

Geeger turns his head and
spots her. She's still over by the
table, slumping toward the trash
can. She looks gloomier than ever.

The sight of Tillie like that
makes the battery in Geeger's
chest go cold.

He turns back to Olivia and
Gabe.

"I WILL *meeet* **YOU AT THE**

CLASS-room," the robot tells them.

He watches them step out into the hallway, then makes his way toward Tillie.

4

Crackle-Crack!

"Greee-**TINGS, BEST FRIEND IN THE MILK-***eee Waaay,"* Geeger greets Tillie.

Tillie looks up at the bot. And her lips, still turned down in a frown, twitch the tiniest bit. It's nothing like the usual grin that Tillie greets him with. *That* grin can make Geeger go from sad to glad in point-zero-six seconds flat!

Geeger leads the way out into the hall. And as he and Tillie head for Ms. Bork's classroom, the wires in his

brain *crackle* with electricity. That happens when Geeger is thinking hard. And right now, Geeger is thinking harder than ever, trying to figure out just why his best friend is so upset.

Crackle!

Geeger has an idea.

"DID YOUR WHY-*errrs* GET TANG-*ulled* UP?" he asks Tillie.

"Huh?" she says, looking up at him.

"OOPS. I *for*-GOT," Geeger

says. **"YOU DO** *nooot* **HAVE ENN-***eee* **WHY-***errrs.*"

Geeger thinks.

Crack-crackle-crack!

"DID YOU CRACK YOUR BRIGHT-*est* **LIGHT BULB?"** Geeger asks, glancing down at the top of Tillie's head.

"OH," he says. **"RIGHT.** *You* **DO NOT HAVE A LIGHT BULB ON YOUR HEAD."**

Geeger thinks.

Crackle-CRACK!

"DID YOUR SER-cuts **O-**ver-**HEAT?"** Geeger asks, eyeing Tillie hopefully.

But then he realizes:

"WAIT. YOU DO nooot **HAVE ENN-**eee **SER-**cuts.**"**

Before Geeger can think of what else that might be upsetting his best friend, however, a third voice enters their conversations.

"Geeger? Tillie?"

It's Ms. Bork. Geeger and Tillie have reached their classroom, and Ms. Bork is standing in the doorway waiting for them.

"Class is about to begin," she tells them. "Please get to your desks."

Ms. Bork steps back into the classroom. Tillie follows after her, her shoulders hunched and her feet dragging.

Geeger watches her go, but stays put in the hallway for a moment longer. And there, he makes a decision. Maybe he can't figure out *why* Tillie is upset—but he *can* do whatever it takes to cheer her up!

Feeling full of **purpose**, Geeger marches into Ms. Bork's classroom and toward his seat.

5

DO NOT WORR-*eee*

Ms. Bork stands at the front of the classroom.

She waits until every last student has sat down at their desk. Then she steps up to the board.

There, she writes down the schedule for the rest of the day.

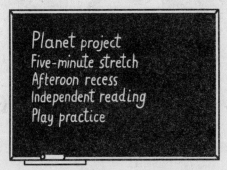

Planet project
Five-minute stretch
Afteroon recess
Independent reading
Play practice

Geeger reads the schedule a few times. All the while, the wires in his brain are *crack-crackling*. What can he do to cheer up Tillie?

"Okay, everyone," says Ms. Bork. "You may go get your projects and supplies."

All the kids hop up out of their seats. Some head for their cubbies to grab their projects, and some hurry for the art supply bins to make sure they get their favorite colored pencils, tubes of glue, and containers of glitter.

All the kids, that is, except *Tillie*. She's still slumped over at her desk. She's just gazing, **glassy-eyed**, at the front of the room.

"DO NOT WORR-*eee*, **TILL-***eee*,**" Geeger tells her, his wires *crack-crack-crackling* in his brain.

"I WILL FETCH YOUR PRO-*ject*

AND SUP-*lieeees.***"**

Geeger lifts his arms into the air. He concentrates . . . and after

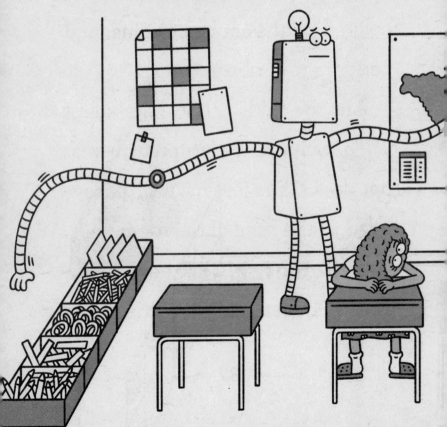

a second, his arms extend. One reaches all the way across the room, over to Tillie's cubby. The other arm reaches all the way across the room in the other direction, over to the art supply bins.

"Check Geeger out!"

Roxy cries.

"*Nice!*" says Raul.

The kids in Geeger's class always love to see the robot use his special skills.

Even Ms. Bork likes it. She's at her desk, reviewing the script for the class play.

But when she hears Roxy and Raul call out, she lifts her head to smile at Geeger and have a look.

Careful not to knock into anyone with his super-stretchy arms, Geeger gently grabs Tillie's planet project from her cubby. He also grabs some art supplies from the bins.

And just a few seconds after Geeger's arms started their journey across the room, they're back at his sides.

Geeger places Tillie's planet project on her desk.

Then, with a **flourish**, he holds his other hand out to her, presenting the art supplies he got for her to use.

There is:

- one mustard-colored colored pencil
  (mustard being Tillie's favorite color)
- one tube of color-changing glue (that
  kind being the most fun to use)
- one container of silver-gold glitter
  (the silver-gold mix being the best to
  make stars sparkling in outer space)

Tillie aims her eyes at the supplies. After a moment, she takes the
mustard-colored pencil and begins

to color the planet on her project.

Geeger watches her closely. Normally, as soon as Tillie gets crayons or markers or colored pencils in her hand, her lips curl up into a **contented** smile. Her tongue pokes out of her mouth as she loses herself in her mark-making. The girl just can't help but be delighted!

But a full minute passes, then another, and then a whole bunch more, and there's no curling lips.

There's no poking tongue. There's not so much as a hint of delight.

Tillie is looking as glum as ever.

And not being able to cheer up his best friend makes *Geeger* feel glum too.

Geeger feels like *crying*—if, that is, his eyes were **capable** of leaking water. Geeger feels like slumping over. He feels like giving up.

But instead of doing any of this, Geeger forces himself to sit up straight.

Because he can't give up on Tillie.

Tillie has never—and *would* never—give up on *him*.

"Okay, class," calls Ms. Bork. She stands up and lifts her arms high over her head. "Time for our afternoon stretch."

Geeger sets the glue and glitter

he's still holding down on his desk. He watches the rest of the kids in the class get to their feet, and then does so himself.

And the movement must jiggle the robot's wires just right, because—

CRACK!

Crackle!

CRACK!

All of a sudden he's got a new idea.

Geeger glances over at Tillie. She's climbing to her feet, moving slowly.

Pretending like he's stretching his neck, Geeger leans in the opposite direction.

"*Pssst!*" he says, grabbing the attention of both Arjun and Roxy.

Arjun holds onto his elbow and yanks his arm across his chest. "What is it, Geeger?" he asks.

"HERE'S A QUES-tion," Geeger says. **"WHAT IS SOME-***thing*

THAT *alll*-**WAYS CHEERS YOU UP?"**

Arjun thinks. Then he drops his arm and says, "Ice cream! Or no—doughnuts! Or no—doughnuts with ice cream on top!"

Geeger frowns. He doesn't have any doughnuts or ice cream.

"I like jokes," Roxy says, swinging her leg back and grabbing hold of her ankle.

"JOKES?" Geeger says.

"Yeah," says Roxy. "Even if

I'm really bummed out, laughing always makes me feel at least a little better."

"JOKES . . . ," Geeger says again. "I *haaave* JOKES."

6

Joke Time

Geeger stands up straight and turns to Tillie. She's finally out of her seat, but hasn't yet begun to stretch.

"*Oooh,* **TILL-***eee*," Geeger says. Tillie doesn't look over. She bends her knees a little and rolls her neck. "Yeah?"

Geeger grins as he asks her, **"WHAT DOES A RO-***bot* **USE TO MAKE NACH-***ooos***?"**

"Um," says Tillie, now rolling her neck in the opposite direction, "I don't know."

"MIC-*rooo* **CHIPS!"** Geeger cries.

Then he waits, knowing that Tillie will **erupt** with laughter any second.

But she doesn't.

All she does is say, "That's a good one."

MIC-rooo CHIPS!

Geeger stares at her, **astonished.** *How can she not be laughing?* he wonders. After all, the joke he just told her is one of the very best he knows.

Then he realizes:

She must have heard that joke before!

Geeger searches his memory banks.

Aha!

"TILL-*eee*,**"** Geeger says. **"HOW DOES A HUN-***greee* **RO-***bot* **EAT DINN-***errr***?"**

Tillie keeps stretching. "How?" she asks.

"WITH MEG-*AAA*-BYTES!"

Geeger cries. Then he reaches his arms out, ready to catch Tillie when she falls off her feet in a fit of laughter.

But she doesn't do any such thing.

She doesn't let out a single giggle.

All she does is say, "Funny."

And even robots know that if a person responds to your joke by saying *that*, they don't actually think your joke is all that funny.

Geeger tries one last time.

"TILL-*eee*," he says. *"Dooo* **YOU KNOW WHAT RO-***bots* **SIT** *on***?"**

"Uh," says Tillie, "chairs?"

"THEIR RO-*BUTTS***!"** Geeger cries.

And Tillie?

All she does is say, "Ha."

Geeger feels confused. And desperate.

He looks around for something

else he can use to try to make Tillie happy—or to least get her to crack a smile.

He spots the glue and the glitter on his desk, the ones he had retrieved for her from the art supply bins and then set aside. Not pausing to think it through, Geeger grabs the glue with one hand and the glitter with the other.

"TILL-*EEE*!" Geeger cries, loud enough to attract the attention of the entire class. **"LOOK AT MEEE!"**

The instant Tillie turns to him, Geeger gives the tube of glue a great big squeeze. With a *POP*, the plastic snaps. A gooey glob of the stuff splashes out and splats across Geeger's face. A second later

Geeger squeezes the container of glitter, and—*CRACK*—a cloud of the sparkly bits explodes into the air.

When it clears, Geeger is left with a dripping, shimmering face.

The room is silent.

Everyone is staring at Geeger.

But at that moment, the robot only cares about Tillie.

He looks at her hopefully—but if anything, Tillie looks **baffled**. She **gapes** at him with her eyebrows perched high on her forehead.

Geeger's wires fizz with an odd energy. The battery in his chest heats up so fast it feels like it might burst.

Geeger has felt a number of not-so-great feelings before. He felt lonely before he started school. And then, on his first day at Amblerville Elementary, he felt nervous.

But now Geeger's feeling something he hasn't before—and it's *really* not-so-great. He feels helpless. And hopeless. And very, *very* frustrated about it.

The next thing he knows, the robot's charging across the classroom, glitter-specked glue dripping from his face and onto the floor. He stomps from one end of the room to the other, then storms right out the door and into the hallway.

7

A Blah Day

Geeger paces up and down the hallway until he hears a door click shut behind him.

Turning around, he sees Ms. Bork. She has a **wad** of wet paper towels in her hand.

She steps up to Geeger and holds the towels out to him.

Geeger takes the towels from his teacher. Then, careful not to get himself too wet—he doesn't

want to rust!—Geeger wipes the glue and glitter off his face. Afterward, he keeps his eyes aimed down, nervous to look up at Ms. Bork. Because he's pretty sure she's going to be angry. Maybe even *very* angry.

After all, Geeger just made a big scene in her classroom. A scene that ended in his leaving the room without getting **permission** to do so.

Not to mention the fact that he

also ruined a tube of Ms. Bork's best glue and a container of her sparkliest glitter.

But when Geeger finally lifts his head, Ms. Bork doesn't look mad.

She looks . . . worried.

"Is everything all right, Geeger?" she asks. "Do you want to talk about what just happened in there?"

Geeger takes a deep breath. Then he explains things to Ms. Bork as best he can. He starts with lunch, sharing how that's when he first noticed how gloomy Tillie seemed.

"I *ah*-TEMP-*ted* TO FIND OUT WHAT WAS *wrooong*," Geeger says. **"I FAILED. THEN I** *ah*-TEMP-*ted* **TO CHEER TILL-*eee* UP. I FAILED AT THAT,** *tooo*. **IT WOULD** *seeem* **I AM** *in*-CAPE-*a*-*bulll* **OF HELP-*ing* MY BEST FRIEND IN THE MILK-*eee Waaay*."**

"Well, that might not have anything to do with you, Geeger," Ms. Bork says. "Sometimes, people just wake up on the wrong side of the bed."

Geeger frowns.

"I DO NOT *sleeep* **IN A BED,"** he says. **"I** *sleeep* **NEXT TO** *myyy* **DIGEST-O-TRON 5000."**

Ms. Bork smiles.

"I don't mean that Tillie might've **literally** woken up on the wrong side of her bed," she says. "It's an expression. A **figure of speech**. What I mean is, some days, you just wake up and feel . . . *blah*."

"BLAH?" Geeger repeats.

Ms. Bork nods. *"Blah.* Down. Bummed out. There isn't always a reason for it. It just is. And it's okay. You're allowed to have an off day every now and then."

Geeger **considers** all this.

"SOME *days . . . ,"* he says.

"Yes?" says Ms. Bork.

"SOME DAYS, I *stiiill* **ACKS-** *uh-***DENT-***uh-leee* **EAT THINGS I AM NOT SUPP-***ooosed* **TO."**

"There you go," Ms. Bork says. "An *off* day. And on days like that, what cheers you up? What makes it better?"

Geeger thinks. And in his head, he sees Tillie. He sees her walk-ing by his side, showing him the best way to get to school. He sees her sitting next to him in class, giving him a thumbs-up just about every time he looks over.

He sees her standing with him

on the playground, explaining the rules of whatever game the kids have decided to play. She's always there, ready to help whenever he needs her.

After giving him time to think, Ms. Bork says, "I sent the rest of the class out to recess. Are you ready to join them?"

Geeger nods, then follows her down the hall and back into the classroom.

8

Here If You Need Me

Back in the classroom, Geeger uses the paper towels Ms. Bork gave him to clean up the glue and glitter he spilled on the floor. Then he heads outside and onto the playground.

There, he spots Tillie right away.

She's not zipping down the slide or climbing through the tunnel. She's not even over in the corner of the basketball court, jumping rope along with Suzie and Mac and Sidney. Instead she's sitting on a bench, all by herself.

Geeger goes over to Tillie. For a minute, he just stands there, not saying a thing.

Then he says, "I *un-der*-STAND *youuu* MAY HAVE *wo*-KEN UP ON *theee* WRONG SIDE OF THE

BED. I *un-der-*STAND *youuu* MAY *beee* HAV-*ing* A BLAH *daaay.*"

Tillie **narrows** her eyes and considers Geeger's words.

"Yeah," she says. "I guess I did. I guess I am."

Then she heaves a sigh.

"I didn't sleep so well," she explains. "Then I got toothpaste all over my favorite T-shirt. Then I bit my tongue during breakfast." Tillie hangs her head. "It's just one of those days."

Geeger sits down next to Tillie
and nods.

"THAT'S OH-*kaaay***,"** he
tells Tillie. **"AND I AM RIGHT**

heeere **IF YOU NEED** *meee.*"

"Thanks, Geeger," Tillie says.

"YOU ARE WEL-*cooome***, BEST FRIEND IN THE MILK-***eee* *Waaay***,"** says Geeger.

Tillie lifts her head and looks at Geeger. And for the first time all day, she smiles at her friend. It's not a big smile. But it's a start.

Word List

ancient (AYN•shint): Very, very, very old

astonished (uh•STAH•nisht): Super surprised or amazed

baffled (BAFF•fuld): Confused by something

brimming (BRIM•ming): Overflowing

capable (CAY•puh•bull): Able

considers (kun•SIH•durs): Thinks about carefully

constructed (kuhn•STRUCK•ted):
Built or put together

contented (kuhn•TEN•ted):
Happy and at peace

erupt (ee•RUPT): Burst out
suddenly

**figure of speech (FIG•yoor UV
SPEECH):** An expression that
uses words in a unique way

flourish (FLER•ish): Showiness
in doing something

gapes (GAYPS): Stares at in
surprise

glassy-eyed (GLASS•ee EYED):

When eyes look shiny or glazed over

literally (LIH•tur•uh•lee):
Actually

narrows (NAY•rows): Makes
less wide

permission (per•MIH•shun):
Approval to do something

pulsing (PULL•sing): Beating
regularly

purpose (PER•pehs): A goal or
reason to do something

realizes (REE•uh•LIES•ez):
Understands

recyclables (re•SYE•cluh•buls):
Things that can be reused in
some form

signaling (SIG•null•ing):
Making a sign that is meant to
start or end an action

striding (STRY•ding): Walking
with long, confident steps

wad (WOD): A thick roll of soft
material

Questions

1. What's your favorite thing to eat for lunch? Do you have the same thing every day, or do you like to switch it up?

2. Do you remember what Tillie's favorite color is? Do you have a favorite color? Has it always been your favorite? What do you like about it?

3. When Tillie draws, she can't help but feel happy. Is there

anything you do that never
fails to cheer you up?

4. Have you ever had a blah day,
as Ms. Bork says? Is there
anything you do to try to get
in a better mood?

5. Have you ever tried to cheer up a
friend? What did you do?

6. Ms. Bork explains to Geeger that
"waking up on the wrong side
of the bed" is an "expression"
or "figure of speech." Do you
know any other expressions or
figures of speech?